(Them Boys: Book 2)

Alexandria House

Pink Cashmere Publishing, LLC
Arkansas, USA

Pink Cashmere Publishing, LLC
pinkcashmerepub@gmail.com

Jah – the Rastafarian name of God.
Jah (or Yah) is also a short form, the
first syllable of Yahweh.

1

Jah

"Yo, Mitchell! Somebody here asking for you!" Poe's voice boomed through the garage.

"Tell 'em I'm busy! Shit!" I yelled in response. Didn't this nigga see me up under this car? I swear I needed to fire his ass, but he was a good mechanic most days.

"It's Genesis."

"Shit, *and?*" I wasn't fucked up about that woman, hadn't been in years.

"And she said Sharpe sent her. Something about his 'Lac."

"Fuck," I muttered, rolling myself from under the car and hopping to my feet.

"Damn, your big ass can move," Poe mumbled as I walked past him, heading from the garage into the office.

This cheating-ass woman looked like she'd always looked—short, thick, fine, and pretty, but she was a damn demon in disguise. I knew that for sure, because that trifling-ass demon had jumped off of her onto me, making me a nigga who didn't love anymore. I just fucked and kept it moving. I had no scruples when it came to pussy.

A smile spread across her face as I moved closer to her.

"Ms. Rykard, what can I do for you?" I asked.

Her smile slid into a smirk. "Ms. Rykard?"

"Yeah. What? You married now or something? You Mrs. Sharpe? That's why you got his car? I know you love fucking my associates."

"No, Jah," she said, as she shook her head. "It's just...when did I become Ms. Rykard to you? And am I supposed to call you Mr. Mitchell now?"

I stepped around her, heading out to the parking lot in front of the building to what I assumed was her new man's car. Knowing she'd followed me outside, I asked, "What's going on with the car?"

"Damn, really? Can you look at me, Jah?"

That's when I knew she was on her usual bullshit. I shook my head as I turned toward her. "Ain't shit wrong with this car, is it? You done drove your ass over here in another nigga's car trying to get some dick from me. I see you ain't changed a bit."

She rolled her eyes. "I ain't fucking Sharpe. I'm working for him. I was running some errands for him, and since I was nearby, I thought I'd drop in to see you."

I smirked. "You miss this dick, don't you?"

"Mm-hmm. Just like you miss this pussy."

"Can't miss what was never mine. That motherfucker belongs to everybody. That's some community pussy."

"Damn, Jah! Really? You still on that? I made a mistake, and I said I was sorry! Shit!"

"Take care, Genesis. Don't fuck Sharpe's car up. And do me a favor, don't come back here. I ain't got time to have to kick Sharpe's ass about you being here and I don't even want you." I said, leaving her outside my shop and returning to my work.

Tricia

It's nothing short of amazing how a man can seem to sense when you get real about leaving him. I mean, I'd finally made up my mind to leave after wasting seven years of my life putting up with his bullshit. I was ready to start over, and all of a damn sudden, this negro became the perfect boyfriend, my dream lover — attentive, no more late nights coming home. Over the last few months, things had been perfect between us, like we'd traveled back in time to when we first got together and he acted like he was so crazy about my ass, convincing me to quit my job so I'd have more time to spend with him. What my stupid ass didn't realize was that it was a trap, his way of handicapping me and making it hard for me to leave him when I became aware of his bullshit.

I fought not to sneer at this man as he sat across from me at the dinner table, inhaling the fried catfish I'd cooked.

"Damn, Trish…baby, this is good! You know you can cook your ass off. Makes me wanna tear that pussy up even more than I was planning to."

Silence from me as I glued my eyes to my own empty plate. Him being nice was really pissing me off.

"What's wrong?"

I glanced up to see his big eyes on me, his eyebrows knitted together. "Nothing, Saul. Just…tired, I guess."

He sat back in his chair and sighed. "I know where this is going. You trying not to fuck? Baby, it's been forever! Shit, it's actually been months! Damn, can I at least put a finger in it?"

Through my own sigh, I said, "Saul, I think I need…I need a break."

"A break? What kind of break?" His voice had risen a couple of octaves. "You tryna leave me?"

He was a handsome man—dark skin, huge expressive eyes, juicy lips, thick coarse hair, and he was a dresser. He was six feet tall, had impeccable hygiene, and honestly, the dick was good. I'd loved him for a long time, had hoped and prayed for this change I saw in him for years, but now, I just couldn't appreciate it.

"No, that's not what I'm saying," I said, shaking my head, and I meant it. I didn't necessarily want to leave him anymore now that he'd changed. I mean, he was my whole life for years. I just...shit, I didn't know what the hell I wanted.

"Then what are you saying? Damn, I'm staying home, doing all the stuff you been fussing about for years, and in return, I can't even get no pussy from my main woman?"

My eyes narrowed at him, and I saw the exact moment he realized his mistake.

"Shit," he muttered. "What I meant to say was—"

"You meant to say what you said. You just didn't mean to say it out loud."

His shoulders fell. "Trish, I love you. Have I fucked up in the past? Yeah. Okay? I have fucked with a lot of women. I'm admitting the shit, but I love you. I ain't never loved nobody but you. I've changed for you. I..." He stood from his chair and walked around the table, stopping next to me and dropping onto one knee. When he produced a ring, my mouth fell open. This was the man who said he'd only get married when his dick stopped working.

"Tricia Shanice Gurley, will you marry me?"

2

Jah

"'Sup, nigga?"

I smiled and shook my head at my brother Shu. He didn't talk all that much, but when he did, just about everybody was "nigga" to him. "'Sup, Shu-Shu? Can't believe you calling me. Your ass off work for once? No double shift?" Me and my brothers all had our own ways of coping with the shit we grew up in. Set fought professionally for years, and now he had his wife to buffer the pain for him. Shu worked all the damn time, and me? I had a whole list of stuff I did to keep from further fucking my life up.

"Just got off working sixteen, tireder than a motherfucker but thought I'd check on my baby brother."

"I'm good, man. Working. You'll never guess who showed up at my shop yesterday."

"Nella?"

"Nope."

"Lanée?"

"Nah."

"Amber?"

"No."

"Not Genesis." I swear he almost raised his voice, and Shu *never* raised his voice.

"Yep, you know she cycles around every few months."

"Man, what'd you put on these women, especially her? Never mind. I don't wanna know. I don't need that kinda trouble."

"Man, me either, especially since she's messing around with Sharpe's ass now."

"Word? She's messing with your boy?"

"Yeah. She says she's working for him, but she came to my shop in his Cadillac."

"Oh, they definitely fucking. You better keep her ass away from you."

"Shit, I intend to. You know I try not to fuck up people I respect. Just ain't right. So what's up with you?"

"Same old shit. Work and…work."

"No new woman?"

"Much as I work? Nah. You? You making you another stalker?"

I laughed. "You got jokes, huh? But nah, not really."

"Not really? Fuck that mean, Jah Rastafari?"

I grinned at his nickname for me. "It means I ain't getting it like Set's getting it. I swear every time I call that nigga he be done just finished fucking. They be getting it in all over that new house in Vegas. Kareema is a G."

"Nah, Kareema was made for that nigga. That's what that is. She's a good one. Set lucked out."

"Yeah, he most definitely did. We all so messed up in the head, I didn't think either of us would ever get married."

"Yeah…"

"Well, thanks for checking on me, big bro."

"No doubt. I'm about to call Set now, see what he's up to."

"Prolly fucking."

We both laughed. Well, *I* laughed and Shu kind of grunted. Then I said, "Holla at you later, Shu-Shu."

We ended the call, and I stared at myself in my dresser mirror. Sitting on my bed, I tried not to think of anything that would put me in a fucked-up mood, but it was too late. My own words had my head tangled up, so I lifted from the bed, grabbed my keys, and headed to the gym before I punched something or someone, and when I got like this, it didn't matter who or what. I was seriously trying not to fuck up an innocent bystander.

3

Tricia

"Thanks, girl! You don't know how much this means to me. I just had to get out of town, or I was going to lose it. You sure your man is okay with me staying here?" I rambled, as I stepped over the threshold of Kareema's and Set's new house. It was so new that the walls were bare, and one of the four bedrooms was still devoid of furniture, according to my friend.

"Set doesn't like people in his space, but I convinced him to be okay with it," she replied, as she grabbed the handle of my rolling suitcase and led me through the huge living room.

"What you convince him with? Pussy?"

"Of course."

"Shit, I think your pussy could convince him to rob a damn bank. That negro loves your ass, with a capital L! Wait, he ain't here, is he?"

"No, *loud ass*, and you need to know that in addition to my pussy, I promised that you'd behave."

I stopped and stared at her as she opened a

door and led me inside a bedroom. "What you mean behave? You act like I be wildin' out or something. All I do is watch TV and be on Facebook."

"I know, but...Set likes peace...and quiet."

"You're calling me loud?!" I shrieked.

In response, Kareema gave me a smirk.

Rolling my eyes, I said, "Is it my fault that I'm passionate? Plus, this mess with Saul got my nerves bad."

She sat on the side of the bed. "Okay, sit down and tell me what he did this time that made you actually leave him."

"The sumbitch asked me to marry him!" I said, propping my hands on my hips.

She frowned. "And that's a problem?"

"Yes! And he's been acting all sweet. No more staying out late; he's hanging around the got damn house all the time..."

"Really? How long has this been going on?"

"Like two damn months! And he's been being so attentive, basically begging for the pussy!"

"Um...aren't all those things that you've been wanting from him? I mean, right before I moved out here with Set, you told me you were tired of playing house with him and that you were ready to get married or break up."

"Yeah, I know, but things...I don't know that I want that anymore. At least not with him." I plopped down on the bed beside her and sighed. "To be honest, I *thought* I was ready to leave him.

Now? I'm just confused. And what am I supposed to do about this whole proposal thing?"

"Uh, you say yes, or you say no. Either you want to marry him, or you don't."

"I don't…I think."

"Trish, what's going on with you? Saul might have put you through some shit, but I always thought you were clear on how you felt about him. What changed that?"

"I don't know. I guess *I* changed, partially because of what you have with Set. The way he loves you, protects you? That's how it's supposed to be. I bet he'd never lie to you."

She smiled. "I don't think he would, either."

"See? Seven years, I've been with Saul for *seven years*, and other than our first year together and these past couple of months, it's been pure fucking torture. The women, the lies, the disrespect…"

"Well, what did you say to him after he proposed?"

"I told him I needed time and space to think. Told him I was going to come out here to visit you for a little while."

"Well, you're welcome to stay as long as you need to," Kareema said sincerely. "And this is Vegas. There's plenty going on here to distract you if you need that."

"Thanks, girl. I truly appreciate it."

*****

What in the fuck is he doing here, in Vegas, in this house? Did Kareema know he was coming out here, too? And if she did, why in the hell didn't she tell me?

Those thoughts screamed in my head when I walked into Kareema's and Set's kitchen. After we chatted, Kareema left me to get settled and I ended up taking a nap, woke up two hours later famished, and followed the aroma of food to the kitchen where I found myself face to face with Jah Mitchell.

Rather than speak to him, I just stood there and stared at him, and he stared right back at me. I felt like a deer in headlights, and then he smiled at me, and I told myself to turn around and leave.

"Tricia? Damn, I thought Set was playing when he said you were here visiting," Jah said. "I'm visiting too."

Before I could reply to that statement, Set waltzed into the kitchen wearing a smile, something I'd rarely seen on his face. He always looked so…scary. "Damn, that smells good! What you got going on in here, Jah?" Set boomed.

Jah was the one cooking?

My eyes skipped over to him as he lifted the lid of a pot for Set to see. Shit, I wanted to see, too, but was too stubborn to move my feet.

"Is that jollof rice? Mannnn, what?!" Set said, sounding like this was something Jah had cooked for him before.

"Yep, and this here is some Gizdodo for that ass," Jah said proudly.

What was with all this damn African food? I hated to admit it, but my ass was intrigued.

Set started rubbing his hands together. "Man, I'ma tear that shit up!" he declared, and then he left the kitchen.

I was about to leave, too, attempt to locate my BFF in the huge house, and interrogate her when Jah's rumbling voice startled me. Instead of the growl that Set possessed, Jah's baritone was smooth but so deep that my belly flipped every time he spoke. And his silly-ass laugh? It could make my heart stop. Plus, the motherfucker was so big and wide and fine. And those eyes? His eyes, adorned with thick brows and lashes, were darker than Set's, and they pierced me as he said, "Wanna taste?"

My eyes darted around the bright kitchen. "Who?"

Those kissable lips of his spread into another smile. Another really nice smile. Then the nigga licked his damn lips, making my pussy purr in approval. "You ever had jollof rice?"

"Uh, no?"

"Wanna taste? I'd really like to know what you think."

"Y'all Nigerian or something?" I asked.

"No, not that I know of."

"How'd you learn to make all that then?"

"From my ex. I made sure she taught me right before I kicked her cheating ass out of my house."

I stared at him again.

"Bring your ass on over here. You know you wanna taste it."

Well, shit, I *did* want to taste it and I needed to stop acting like a lunatic with this man, so I nodded and inched over to the stove, opening my mouth to accept the spoonful he offered me. My taste buds exploded, and I moaned a little.

"Oh-my-gawd! I mean, wow!" I squealed, turning to smile at him, but the look on his face made me quickly back away a bit. He looked like he wanted to tear my ass up right there in that kitchen.

"Good, huh?" he inquired.

"Yeah, it's-it's very good."

"As good as my dick?"

My mouth dropped open, and my eyes raced around the room while my pussy started power walking. "Jah, don't—"

"I know it ain't as good as your pussy. I ain't never had nothing that good before or since. Got damn, Trish, I been missing the shit out of that pussy," he nearly whispered, and then he leaned in close and gently sucked on my bottom lip. A second later, his tongue was in my mouth and my right butt cheek was in his huge hand. Then he dragged his tongue from my mouth to the side of my neck while squeezing my ass.

That damn tongue. That thing had to be made of sin and shame.

"I thought you were mad at me," I managed to utter on a ragged breath.

"I was, but my dick just told me we ain't mad at you no more." He squeezed my right breast through my shirt before leaning in to kiss me again.

"Jah…" I whispered, just before his lips met mine.

"You gonna let me taste that pussy again? Hmm?" He grinned down at me while licking his lips.

In response, I scurried out of that kitchen like it was on fire.

4

Jah

Nine months earlier...

Trisha had a nice vehicle, an Acura MDX. It was spotless, too, inside and out, and that told me she probably had a man. She was giving me a ride home from Kareema's house, my damn hand still hurt from hitting Shawn Thomas's bitch ass, and besides the fact that Tricia was thick as hell and pretty with smooth brown skin and deep dimples and smelled like coconuts, fighting always made me horny, and at that moment, I was working overtime to hide a hard dick.

I just *knew* she had a man, but I needed to find out for sure. If she did, I didn't need that trouble.

"Uh, thanks again for the ride. Nice truck," I said.

"Thank you. I like it." She had a little attitude in her voice, but shit, I liked that in a woman. I was crazy as fuck; a mild-mannered woman wouldn't last long around me.

"Your man got it for you?" I fished.

She rolled her eyes. "Yeah."

Damn. "Smart man. You know I'm a mechanic, right? These are some good vehicles."

She glanced at me. "Good to know he did *this* right."

Awwwww, shit. Sounded like that nigga was on thin ice. My mouth started watering. "Oh, word? Your dude fucking up?"

She sighed. "I've already said too much. We're good."

Fuck. I shrugged. "A'ight."

When we finally made it to my crib, I thanked her again, sat there for a second, and said, "I'ma hop in my truck and follow you home. Ain't safe for you to be driving alone after dark."

Giving me a smirk, she said, "I do a lot of shit alone. I'll be fine."

"I don't doubt that, but I'ma still follow you home."

"No, you're—"

"Got damn! I'm following your ass home and that's it!" I didn't mean to yell, but shit! Stubborn ass…

She rolled her eyes dramatically. "Fine, boy."

I left her truck and headed to mine.

Tricia

I watched Jah Mitchell leave my vehicle and walk to his, and I was so damn glad that negro was out of my space. Jah was undeniably fine and magnetic, big and imposing and I swear he oozed testosterone and a bunch of other shit that had my pussy on high alert. But I had a man, a man I loved, I guess. So many years had passed, and he'd fucked up so many times that I honestly wasn't sure how I felt about him. I suppose I was just comfortable with what we had. I wasn't trying to learn a whole new man at my age.

The rear lights of Jah's truck lit up, and I was just about to back out of his driveway when an alert popped up on my phone from Messenger. I'm not sure why I opened it right at that moment. but I did and damn near dropped my phone. It was a picture of Saul, *my* damn Saul, lying in a bed asleep with his mouth open, a bed other than ours. And he was naked. The pic was from someone named *Nikki ThaBagChaser*, a new Facebook friend of mine, and she captioned it with: *Knocked him out with this pussy. You better come get him before I start riding his face.*

I started to call Saul, but I knew the drill. He'd lie, I'd cry, and a week or two later, neither of us would mention this shit again, because I was too fucking stupid to just leave him or make *him* leave *me*. So I sat there and stared at my phone, nearly jumped out of my skin when a knock came at my driver's side window, and rolled it down to see Jah's concerned face staring at me.

"You a'ight?" he asked, and in response, I started crying.

Ten minutes later, I found myself in Jah's neat living room, sitting on his sofa, waiting for him to return with a glass of water. I had never been in a house so clean. It was literally spotless. It was also the very definition of minimal. Nothing on the walls, no rug on the pristine hardwood floor, and it smelled good, like pine or something.

When he returned with my water, I asked, "You got a maid?"

"Nah," he replied, settling into a recliner across from me.

"Your woman must be a neat freak then."

"No woman right now unless you want the position or something."

I rolled my eyes. "Whatever, boy."

"I like the way you say that."

"Say what?"

"Boy."

"So *you* keep this place clean like this?" I asked, ignoring his sexy ass.

"Yep."

"Wow."

"Why were you crying?"

I set the water on the coffee table and stood. "I'm okay to drive now," I announced.

Without a word, he grabbed a coaster from the opposite end of the rectangular table and set my glass on it. Then he said, "It's got to do with your man? If he ain't treating you right, leave his ass."

"And go where? Do what? I don't have a job." The words had rushed out of my mouth before I realized what I was saying. I stood there startled by my own admission, my eyes on Jah.

"I wanna fuck you," he informed me.

My. God.

My mouth dropped open, and my body? Hell, it felt like it was going to implode. "What?" I asked.

"I wanna fuck you," he repeated.

"But I-I-I have a man."

"I know."

"Uh…"

"I mean, we ain't gotta do it. I just wanted you to know that you got options. You are pretty and fine and sexy as hell, thicker than Texas toast." He licked his lips and then added, "I wonder how you taste. *Shit*."

"You're just trying to make me feel better?" I squeaked.

"Naw, Ma. I most definitely wanna fuck you. My dick was hard just from sitting in that truck next to you. I wanna fuck you in every room of this house, *and* I wanna eat your pussy."

I stood there like a damn statue and stared at him.

He rose to his feet, towering over my five-five frame, looking like he could crush my two hundred and sixty pounds with little effort, as he said, "But if you gotta go, you gotta go. Come on, I'm still gonna follow you home."

I think my brain might have shut down, because the next thing I knew, I'd dropped my keys and was on him, my arms wrapped around his big neck and my lips on his. In a millisecond, my eyes were closed, our tongues were colliding, and a mixture of masculine and feminine groans populated the living room. I involuntarily jacked a leg up around his waist, and then both of my legs were around his waist and he was carrying my big ass through the house, never taking his mouth from mine. I figured out he'd carried me to his bedroom when he gently laid me on a bed. When he ended our kiss, I opened my eyes.

As I tried to slow my breathing, I watched him stand beside the bed and begin to undress, shedding his gray hoodie first and then his sweatpants. Neatly folding his clothes, he turned and placed them on the dresser. Jah was covered in muscles. I doubted there was an ounce of fat on his body.

Shhhhhit!

When he turned to face me again, I let my eyes stroll over his body as he finally took off his blue boxer briefs.

Got dayum!

I swear, my mouth filled with saliva at the sight of his dick. Closing my eyes, I reached down, covered my crotch through my jeans, and softly whispered, "I'm sorry, girl, but you gon' have to take all of that tonight. *All of it*."

"What?" Jah said.

In lieu of an answer, I jumped out of the bed and started shedding my clothes, letting them drop to the floor, and half expected him to fold them for me, but once I was naked, Jah stared at me, rubbed a finger over his top lip, and smiled.

"You are so damn fine, girl. So damn fine…" He grabbed his erection and began stroking it. "You sure you want this dick?"

"You got a rubber?" I asked.

"A whole fucking pack of them."

I crawled back into his bed and was face-down, ass-up as I said, "Then yeah, I'm sure."

I heard him moan, or groan. Maybe it was a snarl, but I know he made a sound, and the next thing I felt was a finger in my pussy and a warm tongue on my clit.

"Fuck!" I yelled. "Shit, boy!"

He licked me from the back for a good two or three minutes and then flipped me over, spread my legs wide, and went back to work, slurping and sucking my clit, two fingers fucking my pussy now, and all I could do was yell and scream, and when the pressure reached its limit and an orgasm seized me, I felt tears rush from my eyes. I opened them in time to see him sheath himself, and then he was on top of me, sucking my neck as he eased the thickest, longest dick I'd ever laid eyes on inside me, slapping his big hand against the mattress beside me and clutching the sheet while shouting, "Got damn, Trish!" against my neck.

"Oh!" I cried. "Oh, oh, ooooh!"

His mouth left my neck, and I heard him croak, "Yeah, baby. Take all this dick."

"Ffffuck, Jah!! Shit!" I replied, as he rocked in and out of me. He wasn't rough. On the contrary, his thrusts were easy and rhythmic, smooth like we were old lovers, and that almost drove me completely insane, because it just felt so good.

As he suckled on my right breast, I felt tears filling my eyes again. The sound of him repeatedly invading my pussy, coupled with the aroma made from the mating of our bodies, in combination with his deep and intoxicating strokes was overwhelming. It was too much, but I wanted it. Hell, I *needed* it.

When I opened my eyes, he was frowning down at me.

"What?" I asked, and then added, "Shit!"

Because…that dick!

"This pussy is too good. I could fuck you all night."

"Then fuck me all night," I whined. "Please fuck me all night."

And he did, stretching my pussy beyond capacity over and over again. He screwed and licked me until I was sore and senseless, and when I finally snuck out of his house, leaving him asleep in his bed the next morning, I could barely walk.

5

Tricia

Now...

Maybe if I'd had sense enough to leave Jah Mitchell alone after that first night all those months ago, Kareema wouldn't have had to drag me out of my assigned bedroom to the dinner table. The food was delicious, and the conversation was lively with Jah and Set doing most of the talking. I don't think I'd ever seen Set smile and laugh so much, but Jah had that effect on people. To be so damn big, he was silly as hell.

I tried not to notice all the messages he got during dinner and how he grinned and shook his head every time he checked his phone. I also tried to convince myself that I wasn't bothered by Set asking him if it was some bitch named Genesis texting him, just like I attempted to persuade myself that I didn't want to crawl under that table and suck his dick. His big, thick, heavy, beautiful dick.

I grabbed my water and took a gulp as I eyed

him in a wife beater, his arms taunting me, reminding me of how strong he was, how I'd showed up at his front door a month after that initial night of dick so good that I'd cut Saul—who thought I'd spent that night with Kareema because that was the lie I told him—off. I couldn't stomach the thought of getting what I'd once thought was good dick when there was some excellent dick across town. So I'd left the comfort of my vast suburban home and driven to Jah's house in a nightgown, coat, and sneakers, hoping he'd be alone, and he was.

When he opened the door for me, I had to force myself not to immediately climb him. He was just so damn sexy.

Looking me up and down, he asked, "Your man fucking up again?"

I didn't answer, feeling stupid that my motives were that obvious. But I guess I didn't need to answer, because he opened the door wider and welcomed me inside. He offered me a seat on his couch, sat down across from me, and without any preamble, asked, "You here to talk or fuck?"

I dropped my eyes and shook my head. "I don't even know."

"Yeah, you do. You just don't wanna say it, but closed mouths don't get fed, Tricia. If you want some dick, tell me you want some dick."

Lifting my eyes, I softly said, "I want some dick, specifically, *your* dick."

He stood, stripped out of the only piece of clothing he wore — boxers — and revealed that damn penis I'd been dreaming about. "What you wanna do with this dick, Tricia?"

I hopped up from that sofa like a crackhead who'd just spotted a big rock on the ground, dropped my coat and gown, kicked out of my shoes, and was on my knees in front of him so quick that it felt like I was outside of my body watching myself. Then I had his dick in my mouth, or at least as much of it as I could take into my mouth, sucking it while moaning loudly.

"Damn, Trish!" he groaned.

I glanced up to see that he had his eyes closed, a deep "V" in his forehead as he gently moved his hips. My mouth grew tired, but I kept sucking. My pussy throbbed, but I kept sucking. Sweat beaded on my forehead, saliva escaped from my mouth and dripped onto the floor, my heart raced in my chest, but still, I slid my hand up and down his shaft and *kept sucking*. He placed his hand on my head, digging his fingers into my braids, pushing my face against the rough hairs above his dick and making me gag on his length, but I didn't care. I wanted him to come; I wanted to swallow his damn unborn babies. I swear I was in a dick-sucking trance or something, so when he backed away from me, taking his dick with him, I groaned in protest.

"Shit, Trish, you gonna make me stalk your ass *and* kill your nigga," he said breathily. "Bend over the couch."

"I wasn't finished," I whined, although my mouth was exhausted.

"I know, but I want that pussy and I want it now. Bend over the couch, Tricia."

I almost fell trying to obey him, tooting my ass up so high that it was actually a damn shame. When he entered me, I yelped. When he reached around and squeezed my breast, I whimpered, "Ooooooo, shhhhhhit!"

"I missed this pussy, baby. I oughta punish your ass for keeping this pussy away from me. Don't you think I should punish you?"

"Mm-hmm." I was high off his sex. I didn't know what I was saying.

"You gonna let me punish you all night?"

"Yes! Please punish me!"

He eased out of me and thrusted back in so hard and fast; my breath got caught in my throat. I heard him suck in a breath and mutter, "Got damn," before thrusting again, and he just kept thrusting deeper and deeper and deeper, so deep that his dick had to be somewhere behind my damn heart.

He fucked me like the ho' I was to leave my man's bed to come screw him. Granted, Saul wasn't home and was most likely out somewhere cheating on me, but this was still a ho' move. Nevertheless, I enjoyed every second of it.

As he pounded into me, grunting and moaning and groaning, filling the room with the sound of his pelvis smacking against mine, I screamed and collapsed onto my knees from where I'd been on my feet, bent over the couch.

"Uh-uh," he grunted. "*Hell*, naw…get up and take this dick, Tricia!"

"Oh, my godddd," I wailed. "I can't get up."

"You done?" he asked. "You don't want no more?"

"I want it. Shit, I *need* it. I just can't get back up."

"Lay on the couch, then," he growled.

I did, and let out a weird gurgling sound when his mouth met my pussy. He licked it, spit on it, fingered it, and was inside me again before I could process what was going on. As I dug my nails into his back, tears flowed from my eyes.

"Why you crying? This dick making you cry, baby?"

"Yyyyes!"

"Want me to stop?"

"Hell no!"

And he didn't.

He. Didn't.

Several minutes later, he had collapsed on top of me, and I was trying to remember how to breathe, when he said, "Don't drive over here in the middle of the night by yourself no more. Call me first. I'll meet you somewhere and we can go to a hotel, or I'll follow you here. This ain't the best neighborhood for you to be driving around in alone at night."

"Jah—"

"I'm not playing with you, Tricia. Call me next time. You hear me?"

"Yes," I whispered.

Jah

I wondered what she was thinking about as she sat at the dinner table staring into space. She was so damn pretty, and I knew for a fact that she had the kind of pussy that makes niggas lose their minds. That would explain why I fucked her all those times knowing she had a damn man. I wasn't proud of myself, hadn't told a soul about it, but I couldn't stop it. And she always smelled so good…and clean. Yeah, I liked shit clean, probably because of my fucked-up childhood. I read somewhere that neat freaks sometimes have a pathological need for control. Well, I definitely didn't control shit as a kid, not while being snatched out of my sleep to rewash all the damn dishes in the cabinets or fight my brothers at the crack of dawn. And I definitely couldn't control my addiction to Tricia. I didn't *want* to control it. I wanted her in my bed every night. I wanted her in my house when I got off work. I wanted her there, naked and wet and waiting for me so we could have sex for dinner. She'd said she didn't have a job, and while that seemed to bother her, it was right up my alley.

"Jah, I might not let you leave when it's time for you to go back home. I didn't know you could cook like this!" Kareema said.

"Aw, this wasn't nothing, sis-in-law. Glad you like it, though," I replied, giving her a smile.

"Yeah, nigga! This shit slaps!" Set said. "Aye, you ready for this week, Rho Beta Gamma man?"

"Hell yeah! We finna show Vegas how it's done!" I answered.

Set grinned. "I know you've been looking forward to this week."

"Yuuup! And don't forget, I got my own table and extra tickets for the public events. You and 'Reema gotta come."

"What I tell you 'bout that 'Reema shit? You think I can't kick your big ass?" Set was crazy as hell, especially when it came to his wife, but I still liked fucking with him.

"Set, stop," Kareema fussed. Turning to me, she added, "We'll be there. I actually can't wait. Oh! Can Trish come?"

I nodded, sliding my eyes to Tricia. "Yeah, she can come. There's a seat for her if she wants it."

On my dick and my face.

Tricia's eyes darted all over my brother's dining room. "Do I have to dress up? I didn't bring anything dressy, so I guess I'll have to pass."

"No, that just gives us an excuse to go shopping. I'm not leaving you here alone. You're coming," Kareema pressed.

Through a sigh, Tricia said, "Fine," and I didn't even try to hide my smile.

Tricia

I lay in bed later that night, wide awake, my mind filled with images of a naked Jah Mitchell. Despite my best efforts, I couldn't stop thinking about him, but I really, *really* wanted to.

Sighing, I shifted from my side to my back and stared at the ceiling. I had my phone on "do not disturb" but decided to check it since I couldn't sleep anyway, finding several missed calls from Saul. Shit, I almost felt sorry for him. He seemed serious about changing, and as he'd said, becoming the man I deserved. I honestly believed he loved me and wanted to do better, but if I was honest with myself, I'd have to admit that I'd cheated my way into feelings for Jah. That, coupled with the fact that I was sure his massive dick had reshaped my vagina, had me basically running from Saul. But what was I running to? Another man I'd have to depend on for support? Someone else I'd be beholden to? I couldn't put myself in that position again, so I just existed in limbo, still connected to Saul while wanting to be connected to Jah, and at the same time, I was trying to find my damn self at forty-two years old.

6

Jah

I was heading to my third meeting of the day when my phone started buzzing in my pocket. I'd been getting and ignoring calls from her all damn morning, but this time, I stepped out the nearest exit and answered it with, "Why the hell do you keep calling me?"

"Because you ain't been answering!" she shrieked.

"What do you want?" I didn't have time to play with her ass.

"Why's your shop closed? I'm in the parking lot right now."

"Why are you at my shop, Genesis?"

"Because I wanted to see you, Jah," she whined.

I smirked. "Damn, Sharpe that bad in bed?"

She sighed. "Wait, you're at the conclave, aren't you? I saw on Facebook that it's this week."

"Look, you know I'm not gonna fuck you, so stop calling," I said, ignoring her question.

"Jah—"

I hung up and was late for the meeting, but shit, I was "The Gawd." Wasn't nobody in my frat gonna check me.

Tricia

Kareema dragged me to so many stores that morning that by the time we sat down to eat lunch, I was exhausted. I liked to shop as much as the next woman, but damn, Kareema had energy for days.

"Girl, what is in Set Mitchell's sperm that's got you trotting around like a teenager? Crack?" I asked, as I dug into my salad. We were at a restaurant inside of a hotel that she said she and Set both loved.

She rolled her eyes at me. "Shut up, Trish."

"No, really though, I'm happy for you. I know I've said it before, but I've gotta say it again. I am truly happy to see you so happy. Love looks great on you, friend."

She smiled. "If anyone had told me my life would look like this right now, that I'd be happily, madly in love with Set Mitchell, I would've been sure they were certifiable grade-a insane, but he's the love of my life with his crazy ass."

"You know what, I wouldn't have believed it either. Set Mitchell? Shoot, I never would've guessed *either one* of those Mitchell boys would be a good catch."

"They're all good guys, just a little rough around the edges."

I shrugged. "I guess. So you still like living here? You don't miss our city at all?"

"I *love* living here, but then again, it's Vegas. What's not to love?"

"Plus, Set is here, huh?"

"Exactly."

"I haven't run into Tori in a minute. She and little Apollo still doing okay?"

"Girl, they're fine. She's upset because I rented my house out to someone other than her, but I don't care. I wasn't letting her move her trifling man into my house."

"I know that's right!"

"Hey, so…back to the Mitchell boys? Jah likes you. You know that, right?"

I dropped my eyes to my salad and frowned. "He's a man. I'm sure he likes anything with a pussy."

"Nah, you must not have seen how he was looking at you during dinner last night."

I shook my head. "I didn't. He was looking at me?" I'd noticed. There wasn't a damn thing about him that I didn't notice when I was in his presence, with his fine ass.

"He was looking at you like he wanted you. No, he was looking at you like he'd already had you, like you belonged to him."

With a smirk, I said, "Now you're tripping."

"No, I'm not. He was giving you the same look his big brother gives me."

"His big brother loves you. You tryna say Jah loves me? We barely know each other." I returned my focus to my food.

When a minute or two passed without Kareema offering a rebuttal, I looked up to see her staring at me, and asked, "What?"

Still nothing from Kareema.

"Don't look at me like that, friend," I practically begged.

She raised her eyebrows.

"Ugh!" I groaned. "Okay, yes, I—we—I fucked Jah. Or maybe I should say he fucked me, because damn, he can manhandle the hell out of my big ass," I rambled.

"I knew there had to be a reason you were suddenly over Saul after all the shit you've been through with him!"

"Yes, I'ma ho', a cheating, lying ho'. I'm not proud of it."

"How long?"

"The first time was that night I gave him a ride home from your house. You know, when Set popped up in town and fucked your baby daddy up?"

"Damn, really?"

I nodded.

"And the most recent time?"

"I don't wanna…can we drop this? I already feel like shit, and now he's sleeping across the hall from me and you talked me into having to be around him at some party and I'm trying to clear my mind right now even though that's damn near impossible with him dripping testosterone all around me. And why didn't you tell me he'd be here, too?"

"I forgot."

"Humph."

"I did! Hey, one last question, is it —"

"It's the best dick I have had in my entire life."

"Better than Basil Banks?"

"Ten times better. I mean, shit…Basil who?"

"Daaaaaamn! It must run in the family."

"Please don't tell Set. He'll think I'ma ho' too."

"Uh, Set brought it up to me last night, asked me if I noticed how y'all act around each other."

"Shit, it's really that obvious?"

"Mm-hmm."

Thankfully, she switched gears after that, gushing about the outfits I'd put together for us. I loved clothes and putting outfits together and never left the house without looking my best. That is, unless I found myself driving across town from the suburbs to the almost hood because I was having a dick fit for Jah David Mitchell. Anyway, that was my only skill, an eye for fashion, and I didn't know anyone who was paying for that, especially from a big girl like me. Hence why I stayed with Saul. He had money, had taken me from a retail job to the position of being his woman. And now? I just didn't know what the fuck to do.

I walked a few paces behind Kareema, Set, and Jah as we approached the Rawley Event Center, my eyes taking in the huge, impressive-looking building. The digital sign out front welcomed the Rho Beta Gamma Fraternity's Annual Conclave in bright red, black, and green lettering. I was so preoccupied that I missed Set and Kareema entering the building, and when I looked up, a very dapper Jah in a black suit, white shirt, and red, green, and black Rho Beta Gamma tie was holding the door open for me.

I gave him a smirk as I sped up my steps. "Dang, boy. You're acting like I'm your date or something."

He slid his eyes appreciatively over my form-fitting black dress and shrugged. "How can I play a position that's already taken, Tricia?"

"Uh…" I said, sounding and feeling dumb. Why had I opened that can of worms?

He rested his hand on my bare back and leaned in close. "It's all right. You might be another man's woman, but that pussy? It belongs to me. I signed my name on that motherfucker."

I just stared at him, mute, because he was right. He'd planted his flag on my pussy the first time he'd touched it.

As he gently grasped my upper arm and led me to our destination, he uttered, "You know what I like most about your pussy?"

"That I keep it clean?"

"That, and that it's so hot and wet. It's always ready for me."

Aaaaaand, there went my panties.

"Aye, man…where your table at?" Set asked.

"Let me go see," Jah replied.

I watched Jah walk away and almost jumped when Set growled, "Kareema said you picked this dress out for her." He shifted his eyes from me to Kareema, licking his lips. "Thank you."

I shook my head. "You're welcome, Set Mitchell. I guess…"

Kareema did look good in a red dress that made her titties pop. I was of the belief that all women should accentuate their assets. My girl had enviable cleavage, so that was her asset. My assets were my legs and ass, so I made sure everything I wore put a spotlight on those areas.

"We're right over here." Jah's voice floated over my head and landed somewhere in my pelvic region. I needed a damn drink.

Once we were settled at the table, I said, "I wonder where the bar is…"

"Me too. Come on, Trish," Kareema said, lifting from her chair.

"Hell naw, what you want? I'll get it. You ain't just gonna be walking around this motherfucker in that dress," Set informed her.

Kareema's mouth fell open. "I thought you liked it!"

"I do."

Kareema rolled her eyes.

"What you want, baby?" Set asked again.

"White wine."

"A'ight."

I'd risen from my seat to follow Set when Jah grabbed my arm and stopped me. "I got you, Trish. What you want?"

I wanted to protest, because this was looking more and more like a date by the second, and I was supposed to be getting my mind right, not going on dates with my cheating partner. But those exotic eyes of his were so damn hypnotic. So I said, "Red wine."

"Okay, be right back."

I reclaimed my seat, and as Kareema complimented me on my dress for the tenth time, I thanked her, but I wasn't in that room with her anymore, at least not mentally. My mind had rewound to my city, to that night two months after the first time I had sex with Jah. A month seemed to be my limit. Once a month hit, the dreams and daydreams and vivid memories would overwhelm me, making it impossible for me to stay away from him. So again, I found myself driving to his house in the middle of the night, but at least I'd managed to put on real clothes this time, stepping onto his front porch in leggings and a hoodie, hoping he didn't have another woman in the bed I craved to be in.

When he opened the door, I breathed my first real breath in what felt like a long time, and softly said, "Hey."

It was after one in the morning, but he didn't look sleepy. He just looked…beautiful, like a big intimidating work of art. Again, he was only wearing boxers, displaying acres of gorgeous brown skin and muscles. His skin was flawless save for the Greek letter branded into his upper right arm.

"Hey," he replied.

"Um, do you…are you busy?"

Shaking his head, he let me into his home, the scent of pine cleaner immediately assaulting my nose. "Were you cleaning this late?" I asked.

No answer as he closed the door.

"I'm sorry for not calling first, but I—"

He grabbed me from behind, squeezing his arms around me while burying his face in the back of my neck, making me shudder and moan as I placed my hands on his thick arms.

"Jah…" I breathed, as he pressed his hard dick against my ass.

Then we were moving. Still behind me, he guided me to his bedroom, to his bed, where he gently pushed me onto it on my stomach. I tried to turn over, but he almost whispered, "Don't move," in an unsteady voice.

So I didn't move.

Climbing into bed with me, he began to rub my back and my ass through my clothes, and it felt so good, so gentle, that as I usually did when I was with him, I felt my eyes begin to well. What was this? I didn't understand the things I felt when I was with Jah. I just knew I'd never felt them before. As much as I loved or thought I loved Saul, I never felt this kind of pull to him. I never felt so addicted. I never—

He began pulling my leggings off, then my panties. "On your knees," he ordered.

And there I was, on this man's bed, ass out, hoodie still covering the top half of my body, scrambling to poke my booty out at him in anticipation of him throttling my pussy. Instead, he spread my butt cheeks farther apart than I thought was possible and literally tongue kissed my ass.

I jumped a little at the unexpected contact, but shit, it felt good. Good and nasty, so all I could do was cry, "Shit, Jah!"

He lavished my ass for what felt like forever,

and then he stopped, climbing out of the bed, and I wasn't sure what to do. Before I could think about it too long, he was back, gripping my ass and sliding that magnificent penis of his inside my pussy with a growl.

"Ohhhhhhh, got damn!" I yelled, sounding as frantic as I felt.

Then he went to work, slow and steady. Stroke after stroke after stroke, I felt myself inching closer to the edge as I reached back to touch him, groping for him while whimpering in pleasure. He leaned over my back, licking my ear and moaning, groaning, crying.

Crying.

He was...*crying*.

And that made *me* cry. So there we were, our bodies mating, our souls crying, and after we somehow managed to climax at the same time and he fell onto his back, I saw the evidence, the tears staining his brown cheeks.

"Jah..." I began.

"Thank you," he muttered.

"You thanking me for my pussy?" I asked, my brows entangled.

He smiled as he wiped his face. "I mean, thank you for that, too, but nah, thanks for answering my call."

"What call?" The hell was he talking about?

"I...shit, never mind. You ain't tryna hear this shit."

"Hear what shit?"

"Fuck," he mumbled. "I…sometimes, I can't sleep. I'm kinda fucked up in the head, you know? Growing up, shit was bad. Anyway, I clean when I can't sleep, but that wasn't helping this time; it didn't make me tired. Fighting helps, but shit, I couldn't go out and just start hitting a motherfucker. I ain't tryna get arrested no more for that shit, so I did like I did when I was a kid. I sat my big ass on that couch and wished someone would come save me." He moved his eyes from the ceiling to my face. "And you did."

"Jah?"

"Yeah?"

"Go brush your teeth so I can kiss you. I can't kiss you with my ass on your breath."

With a chuckle, he said, "A'ight."

After he brushed his teeth, we kissed, and then we spooned. I stayed the whole night, not knowing or caring where Saul was. Jah needed me, so I stayed there with him.

"Tricia? I thought that was you!" A familiar voice brought me back to the present, to that event center in Vegas, in time to see Jah and Set making their way back to our table. I think Kareema had been talking to me, but I hadn't heard a word, too deep into my walk down ho' memory lane.

Frowning, I tried to remember this woman's name, but couldn't, so I said, "Hi, um…"

"Amanda, TK's mom!"

"Oh, yeah!" I said. TK was one of the young guys who worked for Saul, one of the few of his employees I'd actually met. "Hi!" I added.

"I didn't know the mister was a Rho Beta man! I'm here with my oldest son!"

As Jah handed me my drink, I thanked him and told Amanda, "Oh, I'm not here with him."

She eyed Jah as he settled in the chair next to mine. "Oh? Uh…well, you look gorgeous."

"Thank you. So do you."

"Thanks. Well, let me get back to my table."

After Amanda left, a steady flow of obvious Rho Beta men approached the table, excitedly greeting Jah, or as they called him, "The Gawd." Jah was evidently a big thing in his fraternity, judging from all the excitement his presence caused. Once the crowd of his frat brothers died down, I leaned in close to him, and asked, "The Gawd?"

"It was my line name," he explained. "Plus, it's what my government name means—God."

"Oh."

"Fits, don't it?" his conceited ass asked with a grin.

In response, I rolled my eyes, but I had to agree. He *was* a damn gawd.

His phone buzzed and he checked it, grinning as he typed out his reply, and I glared at him.

He finally looked up from his phone and peered at me. "Why you looking at me like that?"

"I ain't looking at you like nothing, just wondering if those hoes text you twenty-four-seven or if they stop to sleep at night?"

"Why it's gotta be a ho' texting me?"

I smirked.

"You jealous, Trish?"

"No," I lied.

"Yeah, okay."

I tore my eyes away from him and scanned the crowd, because I was actually getting heated, and that was pretty damn irrational of me, but that was a bad move. Women all over the room had their eyes on him...or Set. I don't think Kareema noticed since she and Set were all in each other's faces. Shit, they were both gorgeous men, and they oozed danger. Those women probably didn't even realize they were staring at them. So I fixed my eyes on the program sitting before me on the table, squeezed my thighs together, and sighed.

The MC was an actor who'd been big in the nineties. Evidently, he was a Rho Beta man, too. He still looked good, reminding me of the millions of times I'd watched his black love movies. He was in the middle of a joke when what I recognized as the first note of Ginuwine's *Pony* blasted through the speakers and abruptly stopped.

Damn near every man in the room started yelling, "Rhoooooo Beta!" and women started squealing with delight.

"Awwww, shit! Y'all know what time it is!" the MC shouted into the microphone.

I was confused as hell. I didn't go to college, didn't know shit about fraternities, and flinched a little when Jah leaned in and said, "Don't move. If you gotta pee, hold that shit. I don't want you to get kicked."

Kicked?

"What?" had barely left my mouth when *Pony* started playing again, and this time it didn't stop. Men hopped up from their seats, including Jah's mountainous ass, and almost simultaneously hit the floor, hunching it to the rhythm of the song, all while loudly chanting, "Rhoooo Beta! Rhoooooo Beta! Rhoooooo Beta!" Then they all changed up their floor-hunching strokes, lifting a leg as they rolled their bodies against the carpet, and all I could think was, *What. The. Fuck?*

This shit was crazy, crazy and hot. Well, my eyes were pretty much pasted to Jah, so *he* was hot, *really* hot considering I'd experienced those very strokes multiple times.

Mary, mother of God!

With wide eyes, I swung my gaze to Kareema who was dancing in her seat to the music. Set's homicidal ass was staring at her like he was a second from spreading her out on that table. Refocusing my attention on Jah, I licked my lips and rested a hand on my chest.

Damn. Just…damn.

*****

I wasn't sure what woke me up later that night as I slept in Kareema's guest bedroom, but whatever it was also made me climb out of bed and walk across the hall where I gently knocked on Jah's door. Getting no answer, I slowly opened it, stepping inside to see that the bed was empty. Turning to leave, I was startled when I heard, "Don't go." His voice was soft and shaky.

I searched the darkness until I found him, sitting on the floor in a corner.

"Jah?"

"You answered my call again, baby," he said. "You always do."

I didn't know what to say. I just knew he needed me, and something in my soul made me walk over to him, lower myself to the floor beside him, and pull him into my arms where he cried himself to sleep.

7

Jah

When I woke up the next morning, Tricia was gone, and I was in the bed butt-ass naked. It took me a moment to remember her waking me up and coaxing me into bed. Later, the memory of my dick ending up in her mouth rushed back to me, and I think I moaned a little as I chewed my scrambled eggs at the breakfast table. Looking up to see everyone staring at me, I muttered, "What? This shit is good."

"Thank you, Jah," Tricia said with a grin. "You ain't the only one who can cook."

"I see. You got skills, girl. You got skills like a motherfucker."

Tricia, who was sipping on some orange juice, started coughing. I hopped up to pat her back.

"Trish, you all right, girl?" Kareema asked.

She nodded, holding a hand up to me. "I'm fine. Just went down the wrong way."

I took my seat but kept concerned eyes on her.

"Aye, y'all grown, so I don't care about y'all fucking in my house, but got damn, Jah. You were screaming. Scared the shit outta me. It was like four in the morning, man," Set announced all out of the damn blue.

Tricia started choking again, and I jumped up to help her, but she stopped me. "I'm—" *Cough.* "Okay—" *Cough.* "Jah." *Cough.*

"Set!" Kareema shrieked.

"What?" he asked.

I was checking myself in the mirror, about to head out to another day of Rho Beta business, when I heard a knock at my door. My dick jumped at the possibility of it being Tricia, and even though I was the national parliamentarian and had to be present at all the meetings, I was more than willing to be late for some of her.

"Yeah?!" I barked.

The door opened, and I heard, "Damn, nigga, where you find all these suits in your big-ass size?"

Set's ass.

"Fuck you," I replied with a grin. "Ain't you got some squats to do over at that gym? What you lifting now? Two pounds?"

"I'm lifting my wife, nigga. That's what I'm lifting."

I shook my head. "Then why you hating on me and Trish?"

He closed the door. "I was just fucking with you. She a good look for you, with her talking ass, although she be real quiet around you, and she's obviously got you turned out. Had your ass in here howling and shit."

I finally turned to face my older, smaller brother, giving him a smirk. "Again, fuck you."

Set laughed, leaning against the closed door.

I thought for a minute, and asked, "Hey, can I ask you something, man?"

"Depends on what it is."

I chewed on the corner of my mouth. "Uh, Kareema know about the shit Omar put us through?"

He stared at me and slowly nodded. "Yeah. She got my heart. I *had* to tell her."

"What she say when you told her? She didn't...did she look at you different?"

He shook his head. "She looked at me like she cared, like the fact that all that shit happened to me broke her heart."

I nodded. "I ain't never told no one. Not even Genesis, and I was married to her trifling ass."

"You wanna tell Trish?"

I shrugged. "She's got a man."

"Don't look like it to me. The way you look at her? That's the way she looks at you."

"Yeah?"

"Yeah."

I smiled and then dropped it as I asked, "Hey, uh...when's the last time you saw Omar and

Mama?"

"When I scooped Kareema up and brought her here to stay. You?"

"Shit, man…it's been awhile. Can't stand to see the motherfucker like that."

"Yeah, me neither."

*****

The evening event on this day was a performance in honor of our women, known affectionately as the TenderRHOnies. I sat next to Tricia in the auditorium as Kem sang *Love Calls*. Set and Kareema were on the other side of her on the same row, Set's face in his wife's neck. Damn, I was jealous of his ass. He had her with him all the time. I wanted that, too, but not with just anybody. I wanted it with Tricia.

I glanced at her to see her smiling at me, looking too good in an orange jumpsuit that hugged her body. Trish could dress, and I loved that shit. I smiled back at her and returned my attention to the stage. When she grabbed my hand and held it in her lap, my heart skipped about ten beats.

Then my phone buzzed, and as I reached to check it, she glared at me. So I said fuck the phone, kissed her cheek, and kept enjoying the show.

With her.

Tricia

It was late when we all made it back to Set's and Kareema's house, having been serenaded by Kem, Kenny Latimore, and my absolute favorite, the one and only Freddie Jackson. Set and Kareema had already hurried off to bed while I made a pit stop in the kitchen to get a glass of water. I'd assumed Jah had turned in as well, but as I walked down the hall to my room, I saw him standing next to my door. Opening it, I stared at him, and once he walked inside, I followed him, closing and locking the door behind us.

8

Tricia

Lying naked in bed, I stared into the darkness as Jah's body rested against the back of mine and smiled. This felt…right, even though it was supposed to be wrong.

"Omar? My pops? He was mean, abusive to me and my brothers…" Jah began, unprompted. I'd thought maybe he was drifting off until he spoke. Before I could respond, he went on to tell me about his father "training" him and Set and Shu to be men. "Set got the worst of it," he said. "Because he was the oldest, he got the worst of it. But we all got it. I was snatched out of my sleep all the time, jerked to my feet and punched in the chest from the time I was like seven. It happened so much that I was scared to sleep at night, would fall asleep at school. When the teachers called about that, I got my ass beat again, so I'd just…wish myself to sleep, or wish—shit, this is gonna sound fucked up."

"No, it won't. Tell me," I said softly.

His voice wavered. "I would wish he'd pick

Shu or Set. Shit, even my mama, but he never hit her. He respected her too much."

"Jah, you were a kid, a baby. It's okay."

"Nah, it was weak. He was tryna make me strong, but I was so weak…"

I flipped over in the bed and groped until my hands found the sides of his face. "No," I said sternly, "you were a little boy, not a damn man. Your father was wrong. Not you. I know how it can be. Neither of my parents had time to raise me. My granny did, and she's gone now."

"Sorry to hear that."

"Thank you."

"Tricia?"

"Yes?"

"I think I love you."

"Jah—"

"You ain't gotta say nothing. I just…needed to tell you."

"Okay."

After a few moments of silence, I said, "I can't have kids."

"Huh?"

"I've tried, with my—*we* tried. I can get pregnant, but I can't carry a baby to term. My cervix is incompetent, or some shit they told me. I've miscarried five times. The last time, I lost so much blood I had to have a transfusion. The doctors tried medicine to help me hold the baby, but it didn't work. I had my tubes tied, because getting pregnant is actually dangerous for me at this point."

"Oh."

"Um, I could get the tubal ligation reversed and try again, though. There's a procedure they can do. I didn't try it before because I was scared, but I'm willing—"

"Why the fuck would you put yourself through that? Why would you put yourself in danger again?"

"I-I thought…I don't know where this thing between us is going, but you're younger than me and most men want kids. My—he wanted a son. Don't you? I mean, I'll understand—"

"Break up with your nigga."

"Jah, I was talking."

"I ain't tryna hear that shit. You think I'd risk your life for any reason? I'm almost forty-damn years old, not some kid running around trying to plant a damn baby. Old Buddy should've shut that shit down before it got to five times. Losing that many kids wasn't good for your mind *or* your body. Who the fuck puts their woman through that? He had *you*. Fuck a kid. You're enough. You're *everything*."

I was speechless.

So he continued, "Now, back to what I was saying. You need to break up with him. We been fucking for damn near a year now. And even though you called yourself cutting things off last month, we been messing around longer than my marriage lasted. I love you, and I need you in my life full time."

"Jah, I don't have a job or an education. My only skill is buying clothes and putting outfits together. I can't leave one man who is taking care of me just for you to do the same thing. I need to stand on my own two feet for once."

"Okay, you can stand on those motherfuckers at 1891 Garrett Drive."

"Isn't that your address?"

"Yeah."

"Jah—"

"Just think about the moving in with me part right now. But what can't wait is you leaving dude. I don't know shit about him, and I don't wanna know shit about him. I just know I can't share you with him no more. If we gonna do this, we need to do this right."

"Even though it started off wrong?"

"I don't see shit wrong about us being together. What's wrong is you staying with that motherfucker long after it was time to leave. He can't say he never stepped out on you, but I can."

"W-what?"

"I ain't been with another woman since the first time I touched you."

Wrapping my arms around his hard body, I said, "If I break up with him, you gotta break up with whoever the hell keeps texting you."

"A lot of females text me, Trish, but I ain't

fucking none of them."

"Then they need to stop texting you, ASAP, especially Jennifer."

"Who the fuck is Jennifer? I don't know a Jennifer. Wait, I do know one, but she ain't got my number."

"Your ex. The one you and Set were talking about at dinner the other night."

"Genesis? That motherfucker cheated on me with a friend. That's why after I rearranged his face, I put her out my house. I ain't fucked up about her and she knows it."

"Oh…"

"Why you sound like that?"

"I…*I'm* a cheater, remember?"

"Not the same. Your man ain't shit. I am."

"I can't argue with that. But back to the bitches texting you?"

"You breaking up with Old Buddy?"

I didn't answer.

"Look, I get it. You think you owe him for sticking with you even though he didn't get a son out of the deal, or is it because he takes care of you? None of that gave him the right to disrespect you, Tricia. Get rid of his ass. ASAP, as you put it."

"Okay, I will," I said.

"Then consider those other women blocked."

9

Tricia

One month earlier...

What was once a monthly thing — me showing up at his doorstep at all times of night, him welcoming me inside his home, me welcoming him inside of *me* — morphed into a weekly thing six months in, and the deeper I fell in with Jah, the sweeter and more attentive Saul grew. The guilt was cloying, suffocating.

But I still couldn't stop, because I was drawn to the man. Me going to him had ceased being a voluntary action after the first time we were together. It was just...instinct. So for the last two months of our...affair, I made my way to his home every week until one day when instead of showing up at his house after dark, I made a trip to Jah's place of business.

JD's Auto Repair had to be the cleanest mechanic shop I'd ever stepped foot in, from the lobby to what I could see of the garage through the open door that connected the two as I sat and waited for one of his employees to retrieve him. When he walked into the lobby, I think my heart stopped for a few seconds. It wasn't just that he looked delicious in those coveralls, it was the look in his beautiful eyes, like he knew why I was there. I'd already hurt him, and I hadn't said a word.

"Can I help you, Ms. Gurley?" he asked, the pain in his eyes transforming into anger.

Standing from the seat I'd claimed, I moved closer to him. "Ms. Gurley?"

"Yeah."

"Why am I Ms. Gurley now?"

"Because I can tell you're here on some bullshit. Aren't you?"

I sighed. "Jah, I...I'm sorry."

"About what?"

"I-we-I can't see you anymore."

He nodded. "I figured that was why you came here instead of my house. To be honest, I saw this coming, and you needed to stop all that driving alone in the middle of the night shit you kept doing anyway, since you refused to call me."

I could only stare at him because, *what?* He was standing there still concerned about my safety while I dumped him? Now I really felt like shit.

"Thanks for telling me," he added, and then he turned and walked back into the garage.

And me? I climbed in my car and cried all the way home.

That day and all the pain surrounding it played in my head as I sat out on Kareema's patio holding my phone. Considering the fact that what I had with Saul had long evaporated from my heart, having morphed from a love affair to an arrangement, and the love I held for Jah Mitchell, our connection, this should've been easy. But it wasn't. I hated the idea of hurting a man who'd been a part of my life for so many years.

Nevertheless, I called him, holding the phone up to my ear with a trembling hand.

"Hello?" he answered. "Trish?"

"Hey, Saul. You busy?"

"Not too busy to talk to you. How's Vegas?"

"It's really nice. Um, Saul, I need to tell you something."

"Okay…"

"I think we should go our separate ways. I'm-I'm sorry."

"So you done took your ass to Vegas just to break up with me? You fucking somebody out there?! The fuck Kareema's ass got you into?"

"Nothing! It's just time. It's *been* time. Things aren't the same between us and you know it."

"They damn sho' ain't because I been sitting around this got damn house, not doing shit, tryna make you happy. I dropped my hoes for this? Fuck you, Trish!"

He hung up on me and I just sighed, wondering to myself how I ever could've loved a man who'd talk to me like that.

Jah

I held Trish in my arms as we danced to the sounds of the jazz band providing the entertainment for the night's event, a jazz and poetry extravaganza. It felt like we were the only people in the room. I really did love her. I wasn't clear on when I fell, but my ass was on the floor, legs up in the air kicking like a happy-ass dog for her. And it wasn't just the stellar pussy or her booty meat. It was *her*. Something in her soul called to me and connected to my heart. The shit was hard to explain, but I knew she was supposed to be mine and I was supposed to be hers.

I leaned in close and kissed her neck, making her giggle. She said it tickled. So I did it again, making her throw her head back and laugh. Then I kissed her thick lips, and we kept dancing.

Two months earlier…

My past always liked to sneak up on me in the middle of the night, when shit was quiet and peaceful. That's when the demons would pounce, much like Omar. As a kid, I never got to rest. Even when I was big enough to win a fight with my father and he stopped fucking with me, having decided that my training was complete, I never could rest. I'd gotten used to sleeping light, ever ready to be snatched out of bed and have to defend myself or do some shit like mop the kitchen floor at three in the morning. Anything he could think of. I grew up in a twisted boot camp, not a family home.

Some nights, I could shake it off. If I was exhausted enough or had managed to stumble into a fight and kicked somebody's ass, I'd sleep soundly. But on this particular night, the memories and the fear that I'd been trying to shake for decades had a stranglehold on my big ass and wouldn't let go. I was sitting up in my bed, trying to decide if I was going to clean my bathroom or my kitchen, when she knocked on my door. It had happened so many times since we started our thing, I halfway expected her to show up. I swear she had a radar for my pain, or maybe the need for me that was in her was connected to that pain. I didn't know, but I knew the fear left when she walked in my door. And when she looked at me? I believed I could conquer the fucking world, let alone face the demons Omar put on me. We had reached the point that we didn't need any preludes. We each knew what the other required and were more than willing to provide it. So that's what we did.

I carried her to my room, to my bed, and just stared at her, wondering how anyone could step out on a woman so damn beautiful. From her deep-set eyes to her Nubian nose, those juicy lips, and her thick body, Tricia was a walking wet dream, a fucking fantasy come true.

She was staring at me in anticipation, biting her top lip, her hands with those pretty blue fingernails covering her pussy. She'd arrived in a dress and no panties. That dress was up over her soft stomach and my dick was so damn hard; I was sure it could break a cinder block in half.

Licking my lips, I dropped my underwear to the floor and joined her in bed, stretching my body over hers to kiss her lips first, and then her neck, kissing my way down to her plump pussy. I sucked and licked and slurped until she grabbed my head, smashing my face into her sex, making it hard for me to breathe, but I loved that shit. If I died with my head between her legs, then so be it. I'd die a happy man.

Once she finished shaking and screaming, I slid up her body and into her wet pussy, let out a little groan, and worked her like she was a damn sudoku puzzle, closing my eyes and letting myself feel her, *all* of her. I tugged at her nipples, bit her neck, smacked her thighs, ate her pussy again, and when I finally busted, I swear I saw a white light and some angels. That was the second I knew I loved her. After that, she showed up every week, twice one week, and then she ended it. I played hard about it, but that shit broke my heart. It really did.

10

Tricia

Now…

I woke up to the sun in my eyes and Jah's heavy body wrapped around mine. Once I was fully awake, I shook him. "Jah, wake up. Don't you have meetings or something today?"

"Nah," he mumbled, the remnants of sleep heavy in his voice. "No meetings today. Just the golf tournament. I don't play golf."

"Oh? So what you planning on doing today?" I asked.

The next thing I knew, Jah was lifting my leg and filling my yoni. "You," he said directly in my ear.

*****

Set and Kareema opted not to attend that night's event, the national Rho Beta Gamma step

competition. Jah was dressed down in jeans, a
Rho Beta t-shirt, and a Rho Beta bomber jacket
with red Nike's. With his low-cut fade and
stubble-covered chin, he looked so damn good I
had to concentrate on not drooling. I wore a
backless black jumpsuit that dipped to the top of
my ass and black heels, my braids pulled up in a
high bun.

Jah rested his hand on my back as he led me
through the auditorium. When we finally took
our seats near the stage, he leaned in, and said,
"You look fine as hell in this, but if one more of
these niggas looks at your booty, I'ma break
their neck."

"You're gonna break one of your frat brothers'
necks?" I asked.

"If they get down wrong with you? I will
murder their ass with my bare hands, and I'll
smile the whole time I do it."

Staring at him, I said, "O...kay. Um,
Jah...should I be scared of your big ass?"

With a grin, he informed me, "The only thing
you need to be afraid of is this dick."

Rolling my eyes, I said, "I'm thirsty. They
doing concessions?"

"Yeah, what you want?"

"I need to see what they got." I moved to
stand up, and he stopped me.

"Hell, no. You ain't displaying that ass for
these niggas no more. Give me a list or
something. I'll get whatever they got that's on

it."

"Really?" Saul wasn't even this damn possessive and we were together for years.

He just glowered at me.

"Water is fine."

He kissed me and said, "Be right back."

I was people-watching the folks entering the arena when someone said, "Excuse me."

Turning my head to the right, I was met with the smiling face of a young woman wearing a baggy jogging suit. "Hi," I said. "You were speaking to me?"

"Yeah, I was wondering if you have an IG page. I'd love to follow it. I've seen you at other events and you always look so good!"

I got that a lot, other big girls complimenting me on my outfits. "Thank you! I'm on Instagram but I barely post on there."

"Can I get your name on there in case you start sharing outfits or something. You are the bomb! You could be an influencer!"

I gave it to her, and after she left, I sat there thinking about what she'd said. I hadn't thought about anything like that before, but even *I* had to admit that I had a talent for dressing my body. Maybe I could help other women and get paid in the process. Maybe…

When Jah returned, handing me a bottle of water while holding a cup of beer in his other hand, he asked, "Did anybody fuck with you while I was gone?"

"Who would fuck with me, you damn lunatic?"

"A nigga."

"No, Jah. I'm sure they're all too scared of you to actually approach me."

"They better be."

So I *had* noticed some guys looking at me, but I wasn't going to tell this fool that.

The step competition was like nothing I'd seen before. The precision, the athleticism, the absolute pleasure of seeing these young black men committed to something positive — wow! And I can't lie, it was sexy as hell, too. Made me wish I could've seen Jah in action as a young Rho Beta man. Hell, as agile as he was now, I was sure he could still move like that.

Jah left for the restroom, but I was so enthralled with the performances that I barely missed him. However, by the time the last performance was over, Jah still hadn't made it back and I began to wonder if I needed to go find him, but I texted him instead.

Me: *You okay? Do I need to come bail you out of jail or something? Whose ass did you kick in the restroom?*

Jah: *I'm good. See you in a minute.*

Me: *Okay. You better not be somewhere texting bitches.*

Jah: *Never that.*

By the time the winners, who represented the eastern region of the fraternity, were announced, Jah still wasn't back. And I was so worried that I only half paid attention as the young MC said, "As we do every year, we have a group of old heads coming to the stage to show us how it's really done. The Gamma Gamma alumni chapter is about the rip this motherfucking stage up!"

As the arena was filled with loud "Rhooooooo Betas," I pulled my phone out to text Jah again, but something made me look up at the stage, and there he was.

I watched with inflated eyes as Jah and several other men, all wearing black jogging suits and red boots with green bandanas covering their heads, stood stock-still on the stage. *Pony* began to play, and they all hit the floor, making the crowd go wild, including me. After they screwed the stage floor to *Pony*, they hopped to their feet and proceeded to assassinate that damn stage, putting the younger men who'd competed earlier to shame. My mouth probably hung open the entire time, my eyes glued to this man my ho' ass probably didn't deserve as he stepped and clapped. Jah was a huge man, like six-four and over three hundred pounds huge, but he was so light on his feet and so damn sexy and handsome and…shit, was I in love? I really wasn't sure, but I knew I was proud to call him mine. I felt so fortunate that I'd be lying under him that night.

After they finished, Jah returned to me, and I excitedly wrapped my arms around his thick neck and kissed him all over his sweaty face.

In return, he grinned down at me. "You liked it?"

"Hell yeah! Where did these clothes come from?"

"One of the bruhs brought them for me. I wanted to surprise you."

"Well, you succeeded. I loved it, and I love you!" I blurted. Shit, I hadn't meant to say all that, but fuck it. I did love him. I became resolute about it at that very moment.

He dropped the smile he'd been wearing, giving me a look of pure adoration, and then he leaned in and kissed me like my mouth held all the secret treasures in the world. As we ended the kiss and hugged one another, I wondered to myself how I managed to fuck into a real, reciprocated love. Life was nuts.

I squeezed my eyes shut, kissed his salty neck, and then opened my eyes to see TK's mom staring at us. What the fuck was her problem?

11

Jah

"That's all you lifting? How you own a whole gym and you this weak?" I asked.

"Fuck you. I ain't tryna be the Incredible Nigga like you. Your ass literally *stays* in the gym back home."

"Yeah, because I'm tryna stay my ass outta jail. If I don't put that energy into something or some*one,* you know I'ma get in trouble."

"Yeah, kicking asses."

"And any ass will do."

Set chuckled. "You know I know, but uh, you been slacking since you been here. I was shocked you wanted to come to the gym with me today."

I shrugged as I continued to spot my big brother. "I wanted to talk to you."

"About?"

"Marriage."

Set stopped in the middle of his rep. "Marriage? You tryna marry Tricia?"

"I love her, man, more than I ever loved Genesis, and you know how I felt about her."

"Yeah, but don't Trish got a man?"

"Other than me? Not anymore."

"Damn, y'all moving faster than a motherfucker."

"I know. Look, how you making it work with Kareema?"

"Me and Kareema...we just...shit, I don't know. I love her and she loves me. I don't think I could be fucked up enough for her to stop loving me. That's how we make it work. We love each other, and shit, she understands me. You think you got that with Trish?"

"Man, this thing between me and Trish...it's spiritual. We're connected in a crazy way. I can't explain it, but I know it's real. She's why I ain't been in the gym, why I ain't *needed* to be in the gym. She..."

"Calms you? Makes it easier to deal with the bad shit?"

I nodded. "Yeah. Just being around her does that."

"Then she's the one, man."

I smiled. "Yeah, she is."

Sitting in the passenger seat of Set's car holding the breakfast trays we'd picked up for us and our women, I asked, "You expecting more company?" as he pulled into his driveway.

He frowned as he looked at the car parked in front of us. "Naw, looks like a rental. You think Shu done popped up on us?"

"I don't know. The way that nigga works all the time, I doubt it."

We both hopped out of the car, and as we got closer to the house, we could hear voices shouting. I recognized one of the voices as Tricia's. The other was a man's voice.

"You need to leave!" I heard Tricia shriek. "We are over, and nothing is going to change that! Nothing!"

I dropped them damn trays and was about to kick Set's front door in, but he grabbed me and showed me his keys.

"Then unlock the door, nigga!" I thundered.

As soon as he did, I sprinted inside, saw that motherfucker all up in my woman's face, and punched him in the side of his head. He stumbled a little and then fell, so I got down there with him, was about to beat his nose into the back of his brain but stopped when I got a good look at his face. "Saul Sharpe?" I asked.

Holding his head, he said, "Big Nigga?"

12

Jah

Saul Sharpe was well known in our city, the king of his hood with his hands in a little of everything, but giving out personal loans, i.e., loan sharking, had become his biggest hustle. He dealt with drugs and gambling too, though. Saul was a little older than me, and after seeing me beat the brakes off a nigga at a house party for basically no other reason than I felt the urge to fuck somebody up, he hired me to be his enforcer. The job paid well and kept my college dropout ass from being homeless or having to bunk with Set or Shu. Saul was a cool dude, and this position also gave me the opportunity to fight under the protection of his name.

I was twenty when I started working for him, remained his employee for ten years during which I went back to school and trained to be a mechanic before taking the money I'd saved while working for him and opening my shop. Sharpe was good to me. More than an employer, he was a friend, one of my best friends. "Big Nigga" was his nickname for me. Mine for him was always Sharpe. I knew if I needed anything in the world, I could get it from him, and in return for his friendship, I gave him deep discounts when fixing his cars.

We were boys! Hell, I'd texted him and told him about Genesis trying to fuck me, because I thought she was his girl. She was, wasn't she?

Frowning with my fist still in the air, I looked from my old friend to Tricia and back. "The fuck you doing here, man? And why were you in my lady's face?"

"Your—what?!" Still holding the side of his head, he looked up at Tricia. "You been fucking Jah Mitchell?! One of my best friends?! This is the nigga Amanda was talking about? That's why you stopped fucking me? You got-damn bitch!"

I involuntarily punched him in the nose. I think it was a reflex or something because he called my woman a bitch. Tricia and Kareema, who I'd just realized was in the room, both yelled. I growled, "Watch your mouth, muhfucker."

"Damn, Jah!" Sharpe yelled. "How you gonna hit me over what I call my own damn woman?"

"Genesis is your woman, nigga."

"No, she's my side chick. I ain't fucked up about her. I mean, thanks for the heads up, but I'm done with her ass. Trish got my heart."

"So you are *still* cheating?! Wow!" Tricia

yelled. "And here I was feeling all guilty and shit!"

My eyes found their way to Tricia on their own, and I finally asked her, "So this is your nigga?"

The answer was obvious, but shit.

She shook her head. "Not anymore. You are."

Looking down at Sharpe, I said, "Man…shit!"

"Look, man…I don't know what's been going on, but she's *my* woman, been mine for seven years. She thinks it's over, but it ain't never gonna be over. I've changed for her. Gave up having a son for her. She can't fucking leave me! She owes me!"

"Nah, man. Look, I didn't know you were her man, but you fucked up messing around with other chicks. How you gonna say you changed when you just stopped fucking with Genesis?"

"That ain't your got-damn business!" he yelled at me. "I know your ass likes to fight. Shit, that's why I hired you, but you know *I* like to shoot. I will bust a cap in your ass quick if you don't let me up off this floor. Trish, go get your shit so we can go home like I told you to."

"How the fuck you gonna shoot me? Where's your gun?" I asked, flipping him over and patting him down until I found it in the back of his pants. Then I pinned him to the floor with my knee, facedown this time. "Sharpe, I know this is all fucked up, but she's mine now. I ain't letting her go. I wouldn't if I could. I love her."

"Awwww," Kareema sang.

"We getting married," I added, making both Set and Sharpe yell, "What?" while Kareema let out another, "Awwww."

"Married?! I already asked your ass to marry me, Trish! What the fuck?"

"Saul—" Tricia began.

But Sharpe interrupted her with, "You know what? Fuck this! Big Nigga, man…you need to drop her ass! To do this to me after all I did for her? I took care of her!" he yelled into the carpet. "I gave her ass everything! I can't believe this shit, Trish! I stayed with you when I coulda left for a hundred bitches who coulda at least gave me a damn son, you broken pussy bitch! Ain't good for shit! Cheating on me with my damn former employee…"

When I heard him call Tricia, *my* Tricia, a bitch again, I blacked completely out. I legit don't remember what happened right after that. All I know is at some point, Set was basically dragging my ass out of the living room of his house, I could hear Tricia crying, and my hand felt like I'd been punching concrete.

13

Tricia

One hour earlier…

While the men were at the gym, Kareema helped me take a ton of pics that I planned to put on Instagram over the coming days. Then she had breakfast delivered, and I swear I had the best crepe in the history of crepes. Or maybe happiness just made everything taste better.

After the step show, I literally tried to suck the skin off Jah's dick after we climbed into his rental. Seeing him step had my pussy twerking. I was so damn keyed up that I started attacking him before his ass could hit the driver's seat good, had him squealing like an overexcited cheerleader, and when I was done—and he was damn near comatose—he weakly asked, "What the fuck I do to deserve that? Shit!"

"You just…I love you."

"Then marry me."

"Marry you?"

"That's what I said."

This was crazy. I mean, it took Saul seven years to propose, seven years, five miscarriages, a ton of side chicks, and so many lonely nights I'd lost count. It took me cutting the pussy off and basically ignoring him for him to propose, and the kicker? The main reason I stopped having sex with him is because the one time I gave him some after being with Jah, I barely felt his dick. Saul didn't seem to notice the difference, but I did. Jah's humongous dick had stretched my pussy to where it was molded for his dick and only his dick after one time. Well, actually one night, because we screwed until we were too tired to screw that first night.

Those thoughts flowed into others, like the way me and Jah got together and how wrong it was. Wouldn't that doom us? Weren't we destined for trouble? I'd never step out on Jah and I knew it, not because he was…him, but because my heart beat for him. But what if he cheated on me? When Saul did it, it had hurt, but if Jah did it? I didn't even want to think about the pain that would cause, and I knew he had cheating partner contenders. I also knew why. Once you got a taste of him, you were instantly an addict. What Jah brought in the bedroom was rare and hard to find, plus he oozed protectiveness, and with every corner of my heart, I knew he adored me.

"Jah, are you serious?" I asked, pulling myself out of my thoughts.

"Deadass."

I sighed and blinked back tears. Was he crazy? Scratch that—I *knew* he was crazy, but *this* crazy?

"Okay," I said, "I'll marry you."

His eyes went from soft to savage in a second flat, and the next thing I knew, his mouth was on mine, kissing me like the damn barbarian he was.

And I loved it.

I loved every second of it.

After we made it back to Set's and Kareema's, we celebrated our engagement until we both collapsed into an exhausted sleep.

A part of me wanted to tell Kareema about our engagement, although I had no ring to flash yet, but another part of me wanted to keep it between me and Jah, despite the fact that he was probably telling Set at that very moment. Now I understood why Kareema kept what she and Set were doing private for so long. There was something almost magical about two people loving each other *for* each other without outside interference. Right or wrong, we were doing what felt right for us. It didn't matter what anyone else thought, and we were fortunate that there were no prying eyes, nosy ears, or loose lips around to taint what was pure—strange, unconventional, maybe even wrong, but pure.

Me and Jah had a love. A real love.

Awhile after we finished breakfast, I was in my temporary room, smiling at myself in the mirror because I was just so fucking happy, when the doorbell rang. Less than a second later, I got a text from Kareema: *On the toilet. Can you get that?*

Me: *Yep.*

So I left my room, still smiling. At that point, I didn't think anything could wipe that smile off my face. That is, until I opened the door to find Saul standing on the other side.

"Where is he?!" he barked, pushing past me into the house.

"Saul? What the hell?!" was my response.

"TK's mom called me talking about you and some nigga being all hugged up at some damn step show. Where the nigga at?!"

"Damn, you've been fucking TK's mom, too, haven't you? I knew it!"

"I ain't here to discuss who I am or ain't fucking! Where he at!"

"You know what? We ain't discussing shit! You need to leave. *Now!* It's really not a good idea for you to be here, and how the hell did you get this address anyway?"

"Tracked your phone."

"What?!"

"I pay the damn bill, so I tracked it."

"Shit."

"Look, you need to come on home with me before you really fuck things up."

"I broke up with you!"

"Yeah, whatever. Go get your bags. We'll talk

things out. You want a new house? A puppy? Another car? The ring I bought wasn't big enough? What? I'll do it. Just come on!"

He looked so…broken. I'd broken him and I felt like shit. Yes, he'd been a horrible boyfriend, but still, I didn't mean to hurt him although he'd hurt me again and again.

"Saul, I'm sorry. I'm—"

"Who was it, Tri—ohhh, shit." That was Kareema, who entered her living room with wide eyes. "Uh, Saul…you might wanna leave."

"No disrespect, Kareema, but I ain't going nowhere until Trish stops tripping and brings her ass home."

"I'm not leaving, Saul," I informed him.

"Yeah, you are!"

"No, I'm not! You need to leave! We are over and nothing is going to change that! Nothing!"

The next thing I knew, Jah and Set were in the house and Jah had knocked Saul to the damn floor.

Jah
Now…

How the fuck didn't I know that Saul Sharpe

was her man? She'd been with him for seven years? How was it that I'd never seen them out together? I mean, I wasn't the most sociable motherfucker in the world, but I went out from time to time — bars, clubs — and I'd run into Saul a few times, always with a woman but never with Tricia. How was this shit possible? How was it possible that the whole time we were fucking around, I was helping her cheat on Saul Sharpe?

Sitting on the side of the bed, I started calculating shit, trying to figure out how this got by me. Seven years ago…that was right around the time I quit working for Sharpe, so I wasn't around him like I had been. Plus, not only had I never seen them out together, but Sharpe had never mentioned he had a main woman, which Tricia obviously was. It was always other women who brought his cars to be fixed, or, a few years back when I still did a little freelance ass-kicking for him, it would be a male employee of his who gave me the message. Tricia always came to me when we did our thing. I never went to her. It never came up, but I wasn't the type of nigga who'd disrespect a man like that anyway. I'd taken his pussy, snatched it right from under him. That was enough of an assault. I never felt the need to do it in the man's house.

My mind was all tangled up, foggy as hell.

Nothing made sense, and I didn't know what to do with this information. Sharpe and I weren't BFFs or anything. Hell, I couldn't tell you his current address or his damn birthday, couldn't tell you the last time we had a conversation, but we were friends. I didn't do shit like this to my friends, and one thing I despised was a woman who'd fuck a man's friends. Me divorcing Genesis and never looking back was evidence of that.

14

Tricia

Saul finally regained consciousness and left about an hour after Set dragged Jah off of him and out of the living room. I'd cried and lamented and beat myself up, and now I needed to leave Kareema's comforting presence to see what was on Jah's mind besides his next attack on Saul.

The door to his room was ajar enough for me to get a glimpse of him sitting on the side of the bed, facing the window. I knocked on the door and waited for him to acknowledge me. Instead, he sat still, remaining in the same position.

"Jah, can I come in?" I softly asked.

"Yeah," he barked, making me flinch.

So I eased into the room, and rather than sitting beside this angry giant, I opted to sit at the foot of the bed. "Jah, I didn't know you and him were friends. He doesn't really bring his friends around me. I literally only know a couple of the guys who work for him. That's it."

"He never took you out?"

"He did from time to time. He'd take me to these really fancy restaurants mostly. Or shopping, but only after he failed to keep his hoes in check and they called me or something."

"He kept you hidden because of the shit he was doing, the other women." It was a statement rather than a question.

"Yeah. I was feeling guilty and shit about what we were doing, thinking he'd changed, but he hadn't changed. I was a fool to think he would."

"He ever hit you?"

I frowned. "What?"

Silence.

"Once," I said, "but I hit his ass back and that was the end of that."

Glancing over at him, I saw a smile play at his lips. "You still love him? You wanna go back to him?"

"No, I love *you*. I'm where I want to be. I just hope you still want to be with me."

He didn't respond, and my heart dropped to the pit of my stomach. "Jah, um...I'll understand if you want to end things. I'll—maybe I need to be alone for a while. We were moving too fast anyway. I mean, I'm sure I love you, but if you need—"

He reached for me, easily dragging me to him, and fixed his eyes on mine. My heart was hammering furiously from the unexpected action, but I still tried to read what was in his eyes. If he was doing the same, he should've seen fear. Not fear that he'd physically harm me, but fear that he would break my heart.

Just as suddenly as he'd dragged me to him, he stood from the bed, eyes still on me. Then he was climbing on top of me as I involuntarily laid back on the bed. His face hovered over mine as he stared into my eyes again. All I could do was stare back until his eyes left mine as he slid down my body, lifted my skirt, worked my panties down my legs, and buried his face between my thighs. My back lifted from the bed as I clutched the comforter underneath me and sucked in a breath. I wanted to scream, but I also wanted to cry, and at the same time, I wanted to interrogate him, to find out if this meant we were good or if this was a departing, mercy pussy-eating session.

While in my head, I must've tensed up, because Jah used his big hand to spread my thighs wide open, never missing a beat of sucking on my clit.

"Shit!" I hissed.

He squeezed my thighs in his big hands while continuing to lick and suck, and suck and lick as the pressure in my core reached its pinnacle. Then the best feeling in the universe hit me. My breathing halted, my body stiffened, and my entire pelvic region pulsated as my whole body was inundated with an overwhelming orgasm.

My eyes were closed as I softly whimpered and resumed breathing. I couldn't move. Well, I could move my tongue, because when Jah's mouth found mine again, I eagerly put it to work, relishing in the taste of me.

We kissed for what felt like hours, and then he rolled over onto his back, pulling my body against his. Exhausted with emotion and satiation, I soon fell asleep.

About an hour later, I woke up alone. After I got my bearings, I noticed my phone was lying next to me instead of where I'd left it in my room, and on it was a single text message from Jah: *Got a meeting. Be back.*

Jah

The only thought in my mind was how good the lobster was in this place. The steak wasn't half bad either. The beer was nothing to write home about, though.

When he finally arrived, I wiped my hands and gave him a nod, thinking, *Damn, I really fucked his face up.* Dude had knots everywhere.

"The food here is good. You want something?" I offered.

Sharpe shook his head. "Can't chew too good right now."

"Yeah, look, I would apologize for that shit, but you called Tricia a bitch. So on the real, it's your fault I fucked your face up."

He just stared at me for a second before finally saying, "She cheated on me."

"You cheated on her, but she didn't call you a bitch."

"You know that ain't the same. There's levels to this shit. I took care of her, gave her everything she wanted. All her ass had to do was be loyal to me."

I dunked some lobster meat in butter and shook my head. "That's backwards as fuck. You didn't give her everything she wanted, nigga, because I'm sure she wanted *your* loyalty. And if you wanted *her* loyalty, you should've worked to earn that shit a long time ago."

"I didn't earn yours?" he asked.

I shoved the lobster in my mouth and chewed before finally saying, "If I'd known she was supposed to be yours, I never woulda touched her."

"Now you know."

"Yeah, I know."

"*And*, nigga? Now what? You done kicked my ass, and by rights, I should put one in your damn head, but I still see you as a little brother, so I can't."

I sighed. "*And*…I ain't gon' be able to let her go. I can't. I need her, just like you must need my fucking ex-wife. How is you messing around with Genesis any different from me being with Tricia?"

"Because you broke code! I was still with Trish!"

"Shit, ain't not fucking with your boy's ex a part of the code, nigga? You broke that muhfucka too."

"You don't even want Genesis! Trish is my main woman! My main one!"

"She's my *only* woman. All I need is her, and shit, this ain't a damn car we're talking about. She don't want you anymore. You can't have someone who's done with your ass."

I guess he didn't have a rebuttal for that, because he just sat there and stared at me. I stared right back at him.

"Shit, man…I can't go out like this. How is it gon' look for you to be with my woman?" he finally asked.

"Like I said, with me is where she wants to be, so it'll look like she moved the fuck on. Everybody knows about all those other women you got. Hell, I didn't even know she was with you. I doubt if many other people know."

He just shook his head.

"Sharpe, I know this seems fucked up, and maybe it really is, but I love her, so if you can't deal with me and her being together, you might as well shoot me now, but your ass better not miss. You ain't the only one with a gun, not that I'd need one."

He narrowed his eyes at me. "She means more than all these years I had your back?"

"I had your back, too, and you fucked Genesis."

"She's just a woman. Just like Genesis. They ain't shit for us to be beefing over."

"Then let her go."

"I can't."

"Neither can I. So, let's do this."

Sharpe sighed. "Okay. Let's go."

"Just a second," I said, pulling out my phone to text Tricia.

15

Tricia

I love you.

I read that text message about ten times. I could feel Jah's love through those words, but I also felt something else—a sense of finality that made my blood run cold.

I didn't know all the ins and outs of how Saul made his money, because he made sure I didn't, but I wasn't stupid. I knew it wasn't all legal. I knew he was feared by many. I knew he wasn't a nice man, and I knew he had guns, lots of them, not that I believed he flew into Vegas with one of them. He also had connections and a bottomless pit of money. If he wanted someone dead, he could easily have it done, and everything in me told me he wasn't going to rest behind this thing with me and Jah, and I felt like kicking my own ass for putting Jah in this position. He'd beat Saul's whole ass. There was no way Saul wasn't going to retaliate.

I read the message once more before dialing his number.

"Hello? Trish?"

"Don't you do it," was how I responded.
Silence
"Saul, if you ever loved me, you will not harm a hair on Jah Mitchell's head."
More silence.
"You want me? Fine. You can have me, but you have to leave him alone."
"I thought we were over. I thought you didn't want me anymore," he finally said.
"I don't want you, but I can't let you hurt him."
"Trish, I know I fucked up a lot, but I really do love you."
"Okay."
"You ain't gonna say it back?"
"I will if you promise to leave him alone."
"Damn, really? You love him for real, don't you?"
"Yes, I do," I said softly.
And then Saul hung up on me.

*****

I locked myself up in my room and laid in the bed with the covers pulled over my head. I'd tried and failed to get through to Saul, and now guilt had a tight grip on my neck, slowly, steadily squeezing the life out of me. I'd miscalculated, thinking Saul's constant cheating and neglect meant he wouldn't react badly to *my* cheating, and maybe he wouldn't have had I not cheated with someone he considered a friend. Then again, I was attributing a level of maturity to Saul that he didn't possess. What I should've done was left him years ago instead of sticking around for the lifestyle. I should've never dragged another man into this mess, especially not Jah.

Not my Jah.

I couldn't cry, although I wanted to. I—

The doorknob jiggled, and figuring it was just Kareema checking on me again, I didn't move a muscle. I didn't feel like talking to anyone.

"Trish, open the damn door!"

Was I hearing shit now? "Jah?" I called from my spot on the bed.

"You expecting someone else?"

I hopped out of the bed, unlocked the door, and swung it open. There he stood, all big and powerful and beautiful, those eyes narrowed at me. I didn't care about his mean ass scowling. I wrapped my arms around his neck and jumped on him, wrapping my thick thighs around his waist. That made him smile.

"Damn, you act like I been gone forever," he quipped.

After I kissed him, I said, "I thought you were! I thought—never mind. I'm just glad to see you!"

"Yeah? Then why didn't you text me back?"

In response, I kissed him again, then said, "My bad. Carry me to my phone so I can do that."

He did, dropping me on the bed and making me giggle. As he stretched his body over mine, I grabbed my phone from the bed and texted him back: *I love you too.*

16

Jah

We both dressed in black and white for the awards dinner that night, and after all the honors had been handed out, I held my baby in my arms and danced to the cover band's version of The Elements' *Can't Hide Love*.

"When are you gonna tell me what happened?" She stretched up on her toes and spoke directly into my ear.

"What do you mean, baby? What happened when? Where?"

Tricia reclined her head and rolled her eyes at me. "Jah...I know Saul and I know you. I'm sure you met with him today. Didn't you?"

"Did I?"

"Nigga, tell me what happened!"

I chuckled and then pressed my mouth to her ear. "You ever heard of plausible deniability? Let's just say, Sharpe ain't the only one who knows how to buy a gun."

Her mouth dropped open.

"Now be quiet and dance."

She did, but her body was stiff now, so I led

her back to our table.

She threw back a glass of wine and leaned in so close that her perfume filled every inch of my nose. "You killed him?"

"How would you feel if I did?" I whispered back.

"Truth? Relieved. I guess that makes me a bad person, though. Shit, I'm a *horrible* person."

"No you're not, but he ain't dead. We came to an agreement."

"What kind of agreement?"

I told her everything from me buying a gun to me setting up the meeting with Sharpe in the restaurant. I told her what was said and how I left with him in his rental, how we were in that rental when I texted her and had just parked in some remote place when she called. Saul put her on speakerphone, probably not expecting her to beg for my life. By then, everything between us had been settled, but her words? They made me love her even more.

"So that's it? You two came to some agreement and he's letting me go?"

"Yeah, he gets the house. You keep your car…and me."

"And he won't bother us?"

"No, he won't," I assured her.

She nodded, sat there for a minute, and said, "You have something on him, don't you? I bet you have the receipts, too."

"Huh?"

"You worked for him. I bet you know a lot of shit that could ruin him."

I didn't respond, because shit, she had my ass all the way figured out.

"Don't lie, Jah."

"All you need to know is that I love you and there ain't shit I won't do for you."

"I'm right?"

"Not saying. Now tell me you love me back."

"You know I do, but we're not done discussing this. Do you really think this will work? What if he still tries to kill you?"

"You know what? Set was right. You really do talk a lot."

In response, she rolled her eyes and I grinned at her.

"I can't stand your ass," she muttered.

Kissing her neck, I said, "Yes, you can."

"Are you ever gonna tell me if I'm right?"

"Probably not."

"Ugh!"

17

Jah

Four months later...

"Trish, you about ready?" I said, as I walked into my shop's office, wiping my hands on some paper towel. I'd finished my work for the day, taken a piss, and now I was ready to have the roast Trisha had put in the crockpot for dinner and her pussy for dessert.

"Just about, boss," she said.

I grinned when I saw her typing on the computer behind the desk. "What you doing, checking your Instagram on the clock? Gonna get your ass fired."

"You don't even pay me, negro."

I chuckled. "I pay you in dick, baby. I thought you were good with that."

"Oh, I'm more than good with that, and I'm not on IG right now, but did you notice that I have ten thousand followers now?"

"Yeah, I did. You doing it, baby."

"Thanks, baby! Hey, did you see how many likes I got on that outfit of the day post yesterday? I smell a sponsorship on the horizon."

"You see the comment I left on that picture?"

"You mean the one where you advised anyone who read it that, and I quote, 'That's my wife. Don't you motherfuckers look too long'? Yeah, I saw it and deleted it."

"Deleted it?!"

"Yes, I'm tryna get some brand deals. You're gonna have to chill, Jah."

"Whatever. Turn that computer off so we can go. I'm hungrier than ten motherfuckers, baby."

She rolled her eyes. "Boy, calm your ass down. I'll be done in a second."

I reached down and grabbed my dick through my pants. "You know what it does to me when you call me boy…"

She glanced up from the computer and cocked an eyebrow up at me. "Yeah, I know. Hey, can you come here for a minute?"

I moved closer to the counter. "Yeah, baby?"

She rolled her eyes again. "No, come *here*…around the counter."

"Damn, Trish. I'm too tired for this. What is it?"

"Come here and you'll know."

"Fuck," I mumbled, walking around the counter and stopping dead in my tracks as I watched her pull her pants down and step out of them. Then she just stared at me for a second before turning around. She was wearing a damn thong, her ass cheeks were out, and my dick got excited.

"Uh, Trish…baby—"

She pulled the thong off and turned to look at me again. "Where you want it, Jah?"

"Damn, I'm glad you work here with me now," I muttered.

"Really, baby?"

"Yeah, and I'm glad I sent Poe home early."

"Okay, but none of that answers my question."

"Oh." I snatched my pants and underwear down. "You know where I want it."

She smiled at me as she bent over her desk behind the counter, that ass of hers on full display for me. I bit my lip, tucked the bottom of my shirt under my chin, slid my hand over her ass, and eased inside her with a low sigh.

"Ah!" Tricia cried.

I squeezed my eyes shut and sucked in a breath, fighting the desire to nut on contact. "Baby…" I groaned.

"Jah?" she whimpered, as I began to slowly slide in and out of her.

"Yeah, baby?" I grunted.

"Do you know anything about S-Saul Sh-Sharpe being missing?"

She clenched around me, and I tightened my grip on her hips as I stared down at my dick shining with her juices. "Nuh-uh."

Trish slapped the top of the desk and whimpered, "You're lying, aren't you?"

Leaning over her back, I said into her ear, "Plausible deniability, baby."

"Shit, baby! I can't stand you sometimes, Jah David."

As I thrusted deep inside her, making her hiss, I said, "I love you, too."

A southern girl at heart, Alexandria House has an affinity for a good banana pudding, Neo Soul music, and tall black men in suits. When this fashionista is not shopping, she's writing steamy stories about real black love.

Connect with Alexandria!
Email: **msalexhouse@gmail.com**
Website: **http://www.msalexhouse.com/**
Newsletter: **http://eepurl.com/cOUVg5**
Blog: **http://msalexhouse.blogspot.com/**
Facebook: **Alexandria House**
Instagram: **@msalexhouse**
Twitter: **@mzalexhouse**

Also by Alexandria House:

Them Boys Novella Series:
Set
Jah
Shu

The McClain Brothers Series:
Let Me Love You
Let Me Hold You
Let Me Show You
Let Me Free You
Let Me Please You (A McClain Family Novella)

The Strickland Sisters Series:
Stay with Me
Believe in Me
Be with Me

The Love After Series:
Higher Love
Made to Love
Real Love

Short Stories:
New Year, New Boo?

All I Want

Should've Been

Merry Christmas, Baby

Baby, Be Mine

Always My Baby

Text alexhouse to 555888 to be notified of new releases!

Made in the USA
Columbia, SC
25 September 2024

42996753R00061